The World
From My Window

Sheila White Samton

Crown Publishers, Inc.   New York

Published by Crown Publishers, Inc., One Park Avenue, New York, New York 10016
and simultaneously in Canada by General Publishing Company Limited
Manufactured in the Netherlands
CROWN is a trademark of Crown Publishers Inc.

Library of Congress Cataloging in Publication Data
Samton, Sheila.
The world from my window.
Summary: Introduces the numbers one through ten in a rhymed description of the
coming of the night.
1. Children's stories, American. [1. Stories in
rhyme. 2. Night—Fiction. 3. Counting] I. Title.
PZ8.3.S213Wo 1985 [E] 84-21390
ISBN 0-517-55645-6
10 9 8 7 6 5 4 3 2 1
First Edition

for my mother, Irene

The moon is rising in the sky,

One moon.   1

And two pale clouds are drifting by,

Two clouds.   2

And far away, three hills sit back
Against the sky, and they look black.

Three hills.   3

Out of the hills streams spill and flow,

Four streams.   4

Where fish swim high, and fish swim low,

Five fish.   5

Down through the fields the streams cascade,
To where six trees provide some shade.

Six trees.　6

The long-necked cranes in coats of red,

Seven cranes.　7

Talk to the blackbirds overhead,

Eight blackbirds.　8

Who scatter as nine horses run
Across the fields, and day is done.

Nine horses.   9

Night closes 'round the world as I
Count up the stars that dot the sky.

Now if you turn the page and look,
The world will open, like a book.

Ten stars.   10